Bossy Jonathan Fossy

written by
Julie Fulton

illustrated by
Elina Ellis

Jonathan Fossy **was ever** so bossy.
He told everyone what to do.

"Bring me chocolates and gum," he commanded his mum,
"and then paint my whole bedroom bright blue!"

"Tie my shoelaces up! Bring me soup in a cup!
I want squishy fish pudding for tea!"

To his neighbours he cried, "Build a boat ten feet wide and make sure there's a cabin for me!"

When he stood in the square and bossed everyone there it was too much for PC Moran.

At a meeting that night, in the dim candlelight,
the PC hatched a **dastardly** plan.

The very next day, when he set off to play, bossy Jonathan spotted a sign.

WE HAVE FINISHED
YOUR BOAT
IT'S SHIPSHAPE AND AFLOAT
COME AND SAIL
WHILE THE WEATHER IS FINE!

When he got to the beach he let out a **huge** screech -
there were **pirates** all over the place.
There was one with a patch and an earring to match
and a big, ugly scar on his face.

"We require some more crew! I suppose you might do."
He pushed Jonathan up to the ship.
The fierce Pirate Chief roared, "Hurry up! Climb aboard!"
as he curled up his **hairy** top lip.

"The first job on the list," he said, shaking his fist,
"is to cook us a big, **tasty** stew
and then you must clean **all** the pots till they gleam.
Make them sparkle as if they were new!"

As Jonathan rubbed and lathered and scrubbed
he muttered, "This isn't much fun."

But the pirates all sneered and sniggered and jeered,
"Oh! There's plenty more work to be done!"

"Your list doesn't end there, there's a sail to repair,
and the **scuppers** still need **slooshing** out.
All the decks must be swabbed and we want some more grog!
Jump to it and don't mess about!"

"Tie the ropes in a knot! Polish every teapot!
Go and paint our new plank red and blue.
You scurvy landlubber, there's no need to blubber,
that shark will just nibble your shoe!"

Poor old Jonathan moaned and grumbled and groaned.
"Being bossy's not nice, I can see.
I have been a real pain, I won't do it again."

...The fierce Pirate Chief shouted,

"Yippee!"

He pulled off his beard so that everyone cheered.
"Hip hooray! It's turned out as we planned.

We can sail the Fair Lady back to Hamilton Shady.
Let's keep a good look out for land!"

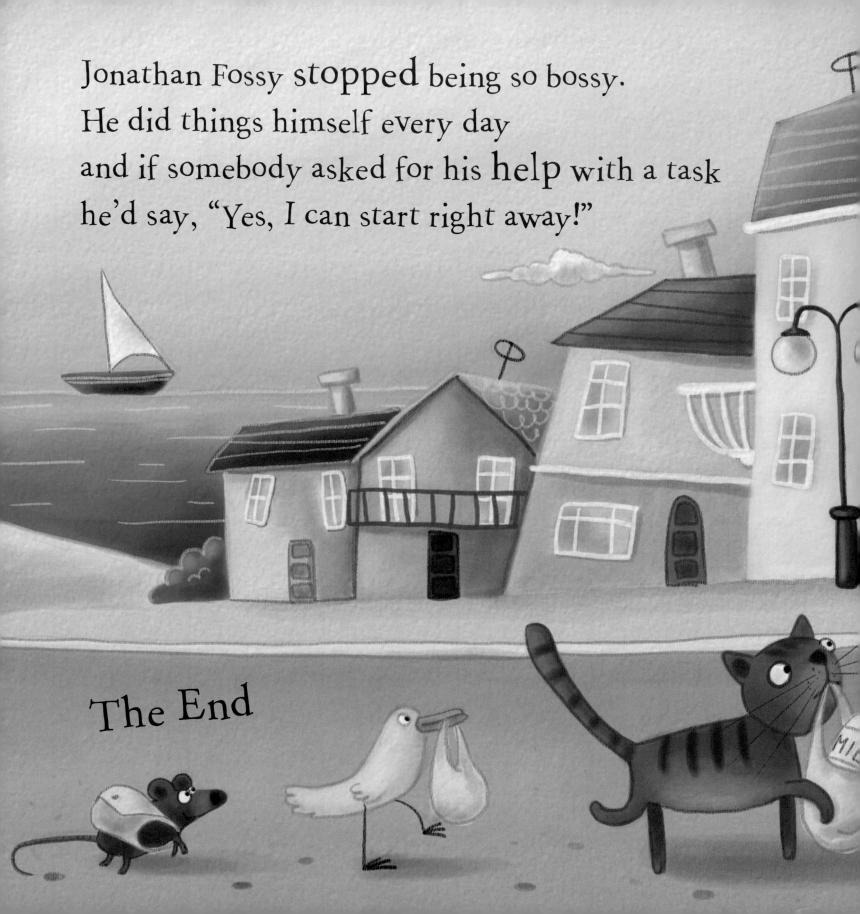

Jonathan Fossy stopped being so bossy.
He did things himself every day
and if somebody asked for his help with a task
he'd say, "Yes, I can start right away!"

The End

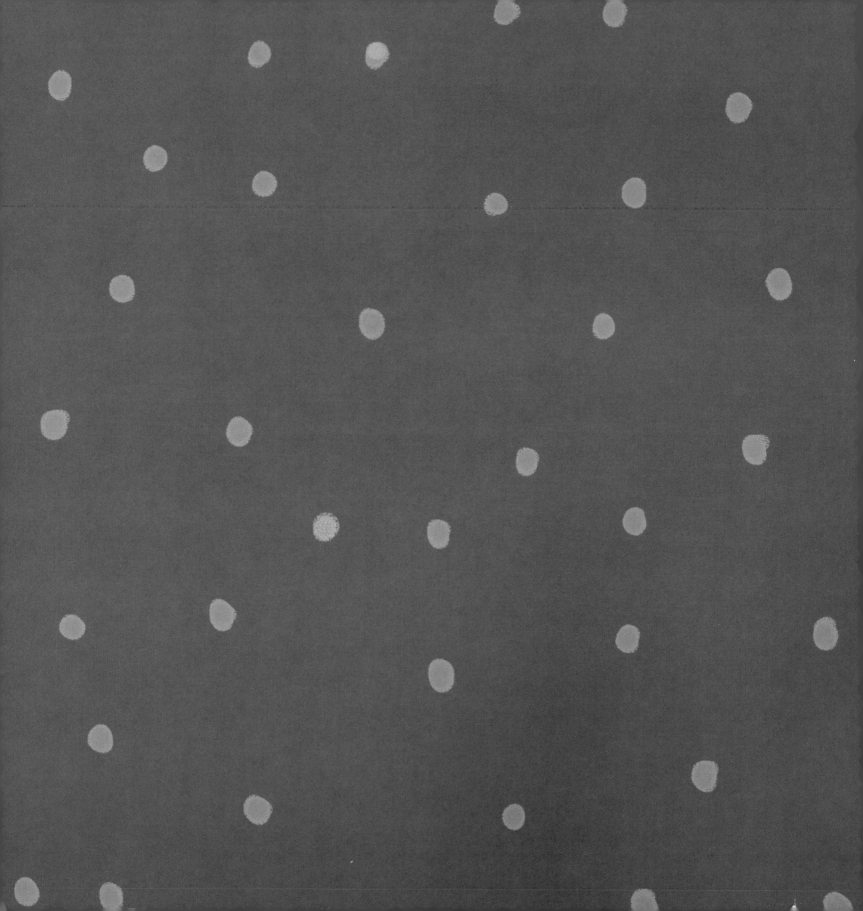

Bossy Jonathan Fossy

An original concept by Julie Fulton

© Julie Fulton

Written by Julie Fulton

Illustrated by Elina Ellis

Published by MAVERICK ARTS PUBLISHING LTD
Studio 3A, City Business Centre, 6 Brighton Road,
Horsham, West Sussex, RH13 5BB
+44 (0)1403 256941
© Maverick Arts Publishing Limited

Published March 2016

*A CIP catalogue record for this book is available
at the British Library.*

ISBN 978-1-84886-186-2

www.maverickbooks.co.uk